Platypus

Also by Joel Allegretti

POETRY

The Body in Equipoise (2015)
Europa/Nippon/New York: Poems/Not-Poems (2012)
Thrum (2010)
Father Silicon (2006)
The Plague Psalms (2000)

FICTION

Our Dolphin (2016)

AS EDITOR

Rabbit Ears: TV Poems (2015)

Platypus

Poems – Prose – Performance Texts

by

Joel Allegretti

The New York Quarterly Foundation, Inc.
New York, New York

NYQ Books™ is an imprint of The New York Quarterly Foundation, Inc.

The New York Quarterly Foundation, Inc.
P. O. Box 2015
Old Chelsea Station
New York, NY 10113

www.nyq.org

Copyright © 2017 by Joel Allegretti

First Edition

Set in New Baskerville

Layout by Raymond P. Hammond

Cover Art and Author Photo by Jon Paul

Library of Congress Control Number: 2017937336

ISBN: 978-1-63045-034-2

Platypus

Contents

IX.

X.

XI.

I.

THE WALT WHITMAN COMPLEX

Go and find a lawn that is as green as "lawn" implies.

Stand at its edge and pluck a blade of grass, only one.

Hold the blade close to your face. Study it. Touch it. Smell it. Experience the meaning of "grass."

When you are sure you know the piece of grass as no one else ever could, put it in your mouth and eat it and, in eating, become the grass.

Walk to the middle of the lawn. Lie down with your arms extended from your side and rest in the knowledge that you are surrounded by family.

II.

AMERICA'S FIRST TELEPHONE DIRECTORY, ANNOTATED 132 YEARS AND 50 ½ WEEKS LATER

***

LIST OF SUBSCRIBERS.

New Haven District Telephone Company.

OFFICE 210 CHAPEL STREET.

February 21, 1878.

Residences.
Rev. JOHN E. TODD.[1]
J. B. CARRINGTON.[2]
H. B. BIGELOW.[3]
C. W. SCRANTON.[4]
GEORGE W. COY.[5]
G. L. FERRIS.[6]
H. P. FROST.[7]
M. F. TYLER.[8]
I. H. BROMLEY.[9]
GEO. E. THOMPSON.[10]
WALTER LEWIS.[11]

Physicians.
Dr. E. L. R. THOMPSON.[12]
Dr. A. E. WINCHELL.[13]
Dr. C. S. THOMPSON, Fair Haven.[14]

Dentists.
Dr. E. S. GAYLORD.[15]
Dr. R. F. BURWELL.[16]

Miscellaneous.
REGISTER PUBLISHING CO.[17]
POLICE OFFICE.[18]
POST OFFICE.[19]
MERCANTILE CLUB.[20]
QUINNIPIAC CLUB.[21]
F. V. McDONALD,[22] Yale News.[23]
SMEDLEY BROS. & CO.[24]
M. F. TYLER,[25] Law Chambers.[26]

Stores, Factories, &c.
O. A. DORMAN.[27]
STONE & CHIDSEY.[28]
NEW HAVEN FLOUR CO.[29] State St.
"   "   "   " Cong. ave.
"   "   "   " Grand St.
"   "   "   Fair Haven.
ENGLISH & MERSICK.[30]
New Haven FOLDING CHAIR CO.[31]
H. HOOKER & CO.[32]
W. A. ENSIGN & SON.[33]
H. B. BIGELOW & CO.[34]
C. COWLES & CO.[35]
C. S. MERSICK & CO.[36]
SPENCER & MATTHEWS.[37]
PAUL ROESSLER.[38]
E. S. WHEELER & CO.[39]
ROLLING MILL CO.[40]
APOTHECARIES HALL.[41]
E. A. GESSNER.[42]
AMERICAN TEA CO.[43]

Meat & Fish Markets
W. H. HITCHINGS, City Market.[44]
GEO. E. LUM.[45]   "   "
A. FOOTE & CO.[46]
STRONG, HART & CO.[47]

Hack and Boarding Stables.
CRUTTENDEN & CARTER.[48]
BARKER & RANSOM.[49]

Office open from 6 A.M. to 2 A.M.
After March 1st, this Office will be open all night[50]

15

[1] Deceased.

[2] Deceased.

[3] Deceased.

[4] Deceased.

[5] Deceased.

[6] Deceased

[7] Deceased.

[8] Deceased.

[9] Deceased.

[10] Deceased.

[11] Deceased.

[12] Deceased.

[13] Deceased.

[14] Deceased.

[15] Deceased.

[16] Deceased.

[17] *New Haven Register,* founded in 1812.

[18] (203) 946-6316

[19] There currently are nine locations in New Haven.

[20] Defunct.

[21] Quinnipiac means "long water land" or "long water country." The Quinnipiacs belong to the Algonquian group of tribes.

[22] Deceased.

[23] First published January 28, 1878. The country's oldest college daily paper, now called *Yale Daily News.*

[24] "Clark Lyman Smedley, an alert and enterprising business man, is the president and treasurer of the Smedley Company and of the firm of Smedley Brothers & Company, engaged in the trucking, moving and storage business in New Haven." Hill, Everett Gleason. *A Modern History of New Haven and Eastern New Haven County,* Volume II. The S. J. Clarke Publishing Company, 1918.

[25] Deceased.

[26] Lawyer.com has a database of 114 law firms in New Haven.

[27] Publisher of *The Poet's Dinner Table,* c. 1875.

[28] Defunct.

[29] Defunct.

[30] *The New York Times,* January 22, 1896.

THREE MEN WERE KILLED

———

Compressed Gas Explodes in a Building
in New-Haven.

———

THE STRUCTURE TOTALLY DESTROYED

———

**Panic Created Among Workingmen
by the Accident—A Section
of the City Shaken by the Shocks.**

NEW-HAVEN, Conn., Jan. 21.—Two explosions started a disastrous fire to-day in the four-story brick building at 72 and 74 Crown Street. Three men were killed. The bodies of the men were removed from the building before nightfall. The dead were:
HAUSER, JOSEPH C., machinist, aged thirty-eight years.
STEPHANS, HARBONA, bookkeeper, aged twenty-four years.
TOOF, The Rev. JOHN THOMAS, aged forty years.

The building was occupied on the two lower floors by English & Mersick, manufacturers of and dealers in carriage hardware.

[31] … and Rocking Chair Co. … and Wheelchair Co.

[32] Carriage manufacturer (defunct), named for Henry Hooker (deceased).

[33] Wooster A. Ensign, dealer in iron and steel goods. "& Son" referred to his eldest boy. Both deceased.

[34] Hobart Baldwin Bigelow, boilermaker and 50th governor of Connecticut. Deceased.

[35] From the home page of www.ccowles.com: "C. Cowles & Company was founded in New Haven, Connecticut over 160 years ago. The company has evolved from a manufacturer of lanterns for horse drawn carriages to a world-class, precision metal stamping company, producing components for U.S. and Japanese automakers."

[36]

[37] Defunct.

[38] Maker of tools for draftsmen and navigators. In 2007, a Roessler-produced brass square in good condition sold for $175. A musician and composer named Paul Roessler, who played guitar and keyboards on the Dead Kennedys album *Fresh Fruit for Rotting Vegetables,* was born in New Haven in 1958, but his website does not indicate whether he is descended from the other Paul Roessler.

[39] The company announced its failure in September 1887. Its liabilities exceeded $1 million.

[40] Four years after E.S. Wheeler & Co. collapsed (see previous endnote), this company suspended business in the wake of a strike precipitated by an attempt to cut wages by 10 to 20 percent. E.S. Wheeler was secretary of the Rolling Mill Co.

[41] Built 16 years after the publication of the first telephone directory, Apothecaries Hall in Waterbury is a historic landmark.

[42] Druggist. Sold saccharin tablets at the rate of $8.87 per pound—in 1913.

[43] The company did not produce pomegranate green tea and vanilla chai.

[44] Defunct. Hitchings is deceased. The Yellow Pages has 164 listings under "Grocery Stores."

[45] See previous endnote.

[46] Not a predecessor of The Foote School, an independent institution of learning for kindergarten through ninth grade, founded in 1916. The school motto is *Laete Cognoscam et Laete Docebo* ("Gladly will I learn and gladly teach").

[47] See endnotes 42 and 43.

[48] Both namesakes deceased. There are 47 boarding farms for horses in the New Haven vicinity.

[49] See previous endnote.

[50] Forerunner of the diner business model?

THE CIRCUS IS COMING TO TOWN

The caravan rolls
Past the Main Street
Piano store.

The elephants
Feel
The chill of death.

BIN-BIN THE DOG-FACED BOY

July Something-or-other, 1930.
Someplace in Ohio, maybe Indiana.

"Good morning," Bin-Bin greeted the fellow in the little wall mirror.
He combed his forehead, ears, cheeks, and neck.
"Give the people what they pay for. A bark here, a growl and a howl there.
That's show biz. I'm worth a hard-earned dime."

They pull in the crowds. Bin-Bin and What Is It?
and Francis-Frances the Extraordinary He + She
and The Countess Ludmilla, all 560 pounds of her,
and her husband, the Human Skeleton,
and the Human Octopus
and the Cyclops of Ceylon
and all the other Boys …
Artie the Alligator Boy
Phillip the Fish-Skin Boy
Cyril the Snake Boy.

In a couple of hours, the rural hordes will tramp the midway to the tent of curiosities,
those peanut-crunching, licorice-chewing, cola-guzzling, jawbreaker-sucking pigeons,
come to stare, gawk, gape, gaze, point, joke, wince, cringe, recoil, and generally look aghast
39 years before Tiny Tim and Miss Vicki
exchanged vows on *The Tonight Show,*
67 years before "My Boyfriend Is a Girl"
aired on Jerry Springer's talk show,
and 80 years before Snooki
inked the contract for her book deal.

THE SEVENTH SON OF A SEVENTH SON

He's a healer. Legends don't lie. He can
    straighten the crooked foot and seal the harelip.
    Seduce the black from a coal miner's lungs and banish the dust to the air.
    Smooth the blistered hand with the words
               "Blisters, leave that hand."

He's a divining rod. Feels the presence of a copper vein in his bones.

He can trace the map of an infant boy's life by the shape of the head. Knows if the child will grow to be lawyer or killer.

He's the hoochie coochie man's older brother and first cousin to the little red rooster.

Conjure Task

Write a 12-bar blues, three stanzas long, using the following seven words:

    Locomotive,
    Longtime,
    Eyes,
    Rain,
    Running,
    Highway,
    Appendectomy.

You may add the articles "a" and "the" and the preposition "like," but nothing else.

When you have completed your lyrics, set them to the tune of "Rollin' and Tumblin'." You'll be following in honored footsteps. Robert Johnson and Willie Dixon, respectively, appropriated it for "If I Had Possession Over Judgment Day" and "Down in the Bottom."

At one minute before midnight, sing your blues. The seventh son of a seventh son will materialize in your home. He'll remain your guest until you write and sing a second blues consisting of the seven assigned words.

A PORCH LIGHT ON A LATE SUMMER EVE

gnat

gnat gnat gnat gnat   gnat gnat   moth

gnat gnat

gnat   gnat gnat gnat   gnat gnat   moth gnat gnat

gnat moth gnat gnat gnat gnat   gnat   gnat gnat gnat   gnat   gnat

gnat gnat gnat   moth   gnat gnat gnat   gnat gnat

moth   gnat gnat gnat   gnat gnat   gnat   gnat gnat

gnat gnat   gnat gnat gnat gnat   moth gnat   gnat gnat   gnat gnat gnat   gnat gnat

gnat gnat gnat gnat gnat   gnat gnat gnat gnat gnat gnat

gnat   gnat   gnat gnat gnat   gnat gnat

gnat gnat gnat gnat   gnat gnat   gnat gnat   gnat gnat gnat   gnat gnat gnat gnat

gnat gnat gnat   moth   gnat   gnat gnat gnat gnat gnat moth

gnat gnat

gnat gnat gnat   gnat gnat   moth gnat

gnat   gnat gnat   gnat gnat gnat   gnat gnat gnat gnat

gnat gnat gnat   gnat gnat gnat gnat gnat gnat

moth gnat

gnat gnat gnat   gnat gnat   gnat   gnat   gnat

moth   gnat gnat gnat gnat gnat   gnat gnat gnat   gnat gnat gnat gnat

gnat gnat gnat   gnat   gnat gnat gnat   gnat

gnat gnat

gnat gnat gnat   gnat gnat   gnat moth gnat

gnat gnat moth gnat   gnat gnat gnat   gnat   gnat gnat gnat gnat

gnat

gnat gnat

gnat

moth

gnat

gnat

gnat

gnat

gnat

I COMFORT CROW JANE

Dear Jane,

                              No one
set the wheat fields ablaze. Look
toward night for the culprits. See
the pockmarks on the black-tar sky?
                              The stars,
numb from the silence of heaven
and tired of being so removed from us,
dislodged themselves and descended
to learn what all the fuss was here.
It was their curiosity ignited the fires
that scorched a path to the sea.
                            The burden
of days blows through our lives
like breath through a harmonica.
In the heart of every tree is a guitar
waiting for its craftsman.
                            The waters
part at our approach. Come. Walk.
Each new era cries for its own Moses.

III.

THE THIRD-FLOOR PROSTITUTES

We called our band the Third-Floor Prostitutes
after the third-floor prostitutes we spied
through the window of a brownstone
across the street from our NY Catholic high school
when *The Godfather* was in theaters.
Our third floor was textbooks and $ax^2 + bx + c = 0$.
Theirs was cold cash and money shots.

The Third-Floor Prostitutes rehearsed
in a West 12th Street basement.
We cut class sometimes, because we figured
that's what the third-floor prostitutes would do
if they walked a block in our size-eight shoes.
We weren't good and couldn't write tunes
worth the money we spent on guitar strings,
but C, F, and G are very forgiving.
We figured if the third-floor prostitutes
heard the Third-Floor Prostitutes,
they'd give us a little action in gratitude
or just to humor us, because how many people
in this world would ever consider paying tribute
to third-floor prostitutes?
We auditioned for school dances,
but three chords played stupidly
didn't have the cachet they have now,
and our name appalled the dance committees.
The Third-Floor Prostitutes were
a dance-banned dance band.

It's forty years later, and the Third-Floor Prostitutes
reunited in a finished basement in Greenwich,
Connecticut, ten feet from the pool table
and one foot from the wet bar.
RÉMY MARTIN FOR EVERYBODY!
PSA tests have replaced A-D-E songs.
The Third-Floor Prostitutes are gray, balding,
and meaty in the midsection.
The third-floor prostitutes are … no doubt … R.I.P.

THE MILK CARTON POEM

During the years John Lindsay, Abe Beame, and Ed Koch
served terms as mayor of New York City

And what happened to

the space cadet in the West 8th Street record store in 1973 who flipped
through a rack of hippie posters and said, "I want it to be odd and sexual,"
while his girlfriend grooved to "Yes We Can Can" by the Pointer Sisters?

And to

the bony black guitar player in Washington Square Park in the late '70s,
the one with the bleach-blond hair, the lavender nail polish, and the red
plastic phallus around his neck, who sang the best version I'd heard of
"All Along the Watchtower"?

And to

the pair of black hustlers who were selling their stuff outside a liquor store
somewhere on the West Side on a Saturday night in '78? Or was it '79?

Where are you now,

'70s Hare Krishna girls who solicited donations in the Port Authority Bus
Terminal?

And where are

the top-and-bottom guys who posed on the cover of a magazine called *Black
Cocks, White Ass* that hung in the display window of a 42nd Street porn shop
in 1980 or so?

What about

the poet who showed up on the subway from time to time in '81, '82, or '83,
the one who said she was trying to raise money to print her work and always
recited the same poem?

And what of

the two white women who boarded a downtown train at 100-Something
Street in the mid-'80s, the ones in the black leather jackets and jeans, one
of whom had lion's-mane hair and a Jack Daniel's face, who told her friend,
"I love the subway; the smell, the odor"—and the other, who pressed the
fingertips of her left hand against the door, stared through the glass at the
tunnel darkness, and let a little softness creep out of her eyes?

TINY LITTLE THINGS

Amoebas, paramecia, and vorticellae,
Coleps, Dileptus, and *Stentor.* They
co-exist by the multitudes in a drop of
pond water. I had protozoa on the brain
one 8 a.m. in a NY subway car, where
there were no empty seats and a man in
a Burberry raincoat stepped on my foot
when the doors opened and he filed out
of my life.

HOW TO COMPOSE A SONATA FOR DOWNTOWN EXPRESS TRAIN

To John Cage

You'll need a portable recording device and $2.75 for New York City subway fare.

Situate yourself at the center of the downtown platform of the 59th Street-Columbus Circle station during morning rush hour. Face the express track and hit "Record" on your device.

You'll hear assorted sounds—downtown local trains pulling in and out of the stop, uptown trains doing the same, musicians playing for spare change, etc.—but these won't be part of the composition until a recorded female voice announces over the sound system, "Ladies and Gentlemen, the next Brooklyn-bound train is now arriving on the express track. Please stand away from the platform edge." The announcement will open the piece.

The A or D train will make the customary subway racket as it charges into the station. The doors won't open noiselessly. A doorbell-type ding-dong will signal they're about to close.

A moment of inactivity will follow. Consider it analogous to a rest in a standard piece of music.

The train in seconds will move out and head for the next stop: 42nd Street-Port Authority Bus Terminal for the A, 7th Avenue for the D.

Remain where you are until you hear the female voice report, "Ladies and Gentlemen, there is a Brooklyn-bound express train one station away."

Turn off your device.

You have finished composing your sonata.

THE MAN-CHURCH REPORT

For Ray Bradbury

NEW YORK CITY – Aired July 17, 2014 – 18:30 ET. THIS IS A RUSH TRANSCRIPT. THIS COPY MAY NOT BE IN ITS FINAL FORM AND MAY BE UPDATED.

ANCHOR: We go now to Washington Square Park, where Erick Torres joins us live.

ERICK: Thanks, Brian. I'm here with Maria Pellegrino of Manhattan, who spent an hour today with an individual who calls himself Man-Church.

MARIA: I called him Man-Church. He said his name was Matt.

ERICK: How would you describe him?

MARIA: About 5'9", slender, red hair in a crew cut, brown eyes, and a soul patch. He wore white cargo pants and shoes that looked like slippers. He said he was 26, but I thought he was closer to my age, 21.

ERICK: How did you meet him?

MARIA: It was on that bench. He was sitting there, listening to a Hare Krishna band. He had removed his shirt because of the heat. I couldn't take my eyes off the beautiful pictures.

ERICK: What can you tell us about these pictures?

MARIA: His skin had become another shirt, all because of the beautiful pictures.

ERICK: What were these pictures?

MARIA: The 14 Stations of the Cross. They covered Matt's entire upper body like a printed fabric. There wasn't an empty patch of skin below his neck, except for his hands. Even his armpits were shaved and beautified with pictures. The first station, "Jesus Is Condemned to Death," covered half his back, from the right shoulder blade down to the waist. His chest and belly were the canvas for the twelfth station, "Jesus Dies on the Cross." His nipples doubled as the nails.

ERICK: You're saying his entire body was tattooed?

MARIA: The pictures were too beautiful to be called tattoos. I'm studying art history at NYU. They were like El Greco oils, but in ink. I sat down and struck up a conversation. I asked why the Stations of the Cross. Matt just smiled—the braces on his teeth surprised me—and asked, "You like them?" I said I did. He wanted to know if I had a favorite one.

31

ERICK: Did you?

MARIA: The fourth station, "Jesus Meets His Mother." I lost my mother when I
             was 15. The Blessed Mother's face occupied his right bicep. I saw my
             mother's eyes in Mary's eyes. Her veil was Yves Klein's blue. A run-of-
             the-mill tattoo artist wouldn't use that blue. He wouldn't know it. I had to
             touch Matt's arm, because the veil looked like real cloth.

ERICK: What else did you talk about?

MARIA: All we talked about were the beautiful pictures. I didn't ask him where he
             lived or what he did with his life. For the time we were together, only the
             beautiful pictures mattered. I wanted to photograph his body gallery, but
             he raised both hands. He reacted as if I had threatened him. He was
             adamant.

ERICK: Why?

MARIA: I don't know. I respected his privacy, even though by taking off his shirt in
             the park, he had forfeited his privacy.

ERICK: How did you two part?

MARIA: The same ordinary way thousands of other people in New York part. Matt
             asked me to walk him to the subway. I said yes, of course. He balled up
             his shirt and carried it in his left hand as we strolled up to Broadway and
             then walked the 10 blocks to the Union Square station. Everybody we
             passed took notice of the pictures. In a city where tattoos are as plentiful
             as college graduates with communications degrees, people gaped like
             Munch's *Scream*, which ought to tell you how rarefied the beautiful
             pictures were. I felt betrayed. Strangers' eyes were luxuriating in what I
             decided was rightfully mine. You can understand, can't you? I'm the one
             who had engaged him in conversation about the beautiful pictures. *They*
             didn't.

             Matt must have sensed my displeasure. He shook out his long-sleeve shirt
             and put it on. It was a Brad Paisley T-shirt. When we reached the subway
             station, I told him I wanted to see him again. That's when I called him
             Man-Church, kind of like a pet name.

ERICK: What was his answer?

MARIA: Silence and a polite smile. He shook his head. My disappointment was visible. I made sure of it. I said I'd like to see the Virgin one last time. Matt pulled off his shirt and turned his naked shoulder to me, almost like a model. I had the urge to kiss it, but I restrained myself. "It was nice talking to you, Maria," he said and scooted down the stairs. I followed him, because I wanted to see which direction he'd go in. I didn't expect him to head to the uptown platform. I figured somebody like Matt lived in Brooklyn. I was tempted to hop on his train.

I can't stop thinking about him. I can't stop thinking about the beautiful pictures. I didn't even realize I was in Washington Square Park again until I saw the arch. I'm sure I'll come back tomorrow and hope he'll be here.

ERICK: How do you feel now?

MARIA: Saved, I think. Yes, I feel saved.

ERICK: Brian, back to you.

###

DEPOSITION: ARCHAEOPTERYX

I'm evolution's transgender paradigm. Dinosaur? Bird? My name, a language hybrid (New Latin, from Greek, *ancient wing*), tells nothing. It could apply to the pteranodon and *Rhamphorhynchus*. I'm said to be extinct. Perish the thought. The coelacanth was presumed gone for good by the Late Cretaceous period. That is, until 1938, when South African fishermen netted one of the nasty-looking things in the Indian Ocean.

I in my Jurassic days may have lived in what is now Bavaria, but New York's Central Park is my present residence of choice. I favor one particular branch of one particular tree, from which I can see the Dakota. I have hope upon hope that I'll catch a glimpse of Yoko, but she must leave by limo. Joggers and casual walkers see me, but must take me for a mutant parrot or whatnot.

I leave the park from time to time. I'm drawn as if by magnet to the American Museum of Natural History and flap around the grounds.

I'm not a fossil. Never was. I am very much alive. I'm alive. I'm alive. I'm alive.

*

The paramedics hoisted the stretcher into the ambulance, climbed in the back, and pulled the doors shut.

"Damn, she's heavy," one said. "She's built like a trucker."

"Pre-op transsexual," said the other, looking at the covered body, adding, "a deranged pre-op transsexual."

"Obviously."

"According to the cop, the woman who lives in the apartment next door said she heard this one yell, 'I'm alive, I'm alive,' and then"—he snapped his fingers—"out the window."

"Sounds like drugs were in there somewhere."

"It wouldn't be the first time. We'll know either way when the toxicology report is in. The neighbors said he—she had a PhD."

"A lot of good it did her."

The ambulance turned the corner and sped up the avenue. The cars veered off to the side to let it pass.

34

THE BOWERY (NOT)SONNET

Tell me everything you know about a green door on Bleecker Street;
Not about the diligent carpenter who planed it into being,
But the door itself and its need to separate us from someone else.
Tell me when the Bouwerie dropped its UIE and gave up its CBGB.

Then I will tell you I want to spend a night—or maybe two—
In a seaman's home on 4th Street and imagine a concertina
Wheezing me to sleep with choruses of "Sail Away, Ladies."
But right now, I'm distracted by the man on the fire escape

Who is facing lower Manhattan. He is, I suppose, thinking
About the Twin Towers and how loss makes us who we are.
7 OUT OF EVERY 10 9/11 FIRST RESPONDERS SUFFER FROM RESPIRATORY DISTRESS.*
He's smoking a cigar; even minor acts show we're engaged in life.

Meanwhile, over on East 7th Christ looks down
On McSorley's Old Ale House and smiles at the goodness of it all.

* From a placard posted along the Bowery in May 2007

IV.

IT'S ALWAYS PRIME TIME
For 5 Voices

Voice 1:   The mirror on the bathroom medicine cabinet is your ultimate television set.
Voice 2:   In a moment the present will join the past, and you will have one more regret.
Voice 3:   If a tree falls in the forest, do the other trees know it?
Voice 4:   Would a cobra be less of a cobra if it were called a peacock?
Voice 5:   In 27 minutes you will be beautiful again.

Voice 3:   If a tree falls in the forest, do the other trees know it?
Voice 5:   In 27 minutes you will be beautiful again.
Voice 2:   In a moment the present will join the past, and you will have one more regret.
Voice 1:   The mirror on the bathroom medicine cabinet is your ultimate television set.
Voice 4:   Would a cobra be less of a cobra if it were called a peacock?

Voice 2:   In a moment the present will join the past, and you will have one more regret.
Voice 4:   Would a cobra be less of a cobra if it were called a peacock?
Voice 5:   In 27 minutes you will be beautiful again.
Voice 3:   If a tree falls in the forest, do the other trees know it?
Voice 1:   The mirror on the bathroom medicine cabinet is your ultimate television set.

Voice 5:   In 27 minutes you will be beautiful again.
Voice 1:   The mirror on the bathroom medicine cabinet is your ultimate television set.
Voice 4:   Would a cobra be less of a cobra if it were called a peacock?
Voice 2:   In a moment the present will join the past, and you will have one more regret.
Voice 3:   If a tree falls in the forest, do the other trees know it?

Voice 4:   Would a cobra be less of a cobra if it were called a peacock?
Voice 3:   If a tree falls in the forest, do the other trees know it?
Voice 1:   The mirror on the bathroom medicine cabinet is your ultimate television set.
Voice 5:   In 27 minutes you will be beautiful again.
Voice 2:   In a moment the present will join the past, and you will have one more regret.

Voice 1:   The mirror on the bathroom medicine cabinet is your ultimate television set.
Voice 2:   In a moment the present will join the past, and you will have one more regret.
Voice 3:   If a tree falls in the forest, do the other trees know it?
Voice 4:   Would a cobra be less of a cobra if it were called a peacock?
Voice 5:   In 27 minutes you will be beautiful again.

THE BOB CRANE POEM

A single hit TV series that's older
than the Beatles' breakup,
a bit part on Dick Van Dyke's show,
a supporting role on Donna Reed's,
a one-star Disney movie.

You, Bob, were footnote bound,
but sex and murder kept you in the text.
You were luckier than most, though.
You rated a bio-pic, and let's be honest.
Greg Kinnear is better looking.

THE LIBERACE POEM

After watching Michael Douglas
in *Behind the Candelabra*

it's about ME
and ME and,
oh yes, ME;
it's about you
as long as you
are about ME;
you'll be MY
mirror: reflect
what I am.

THE LINDA WOLFE POEM

A resident of Anderson, Indiana, who holds
the world record for most-married woman

I do believe I meant "I do" the first time I said "I do"
and discovered I didn't mean "I do" and thought my
second "I do" would be my last "I do," but another
"I do" was in the cards, followed by a fourth "I do,"
and then a fifth, and then … I do like the words "I do"
and am more adept at saying "I do" than others are at
saying "I do," if I do say so myself, because I've said
"I do" even more than Zsa Zsa, who multiplied "I do"
by nine, and I do have to admit that I do think of her
as an "I do" amateur. Yes, I do. I do hope my latest
"I do" will be my final "I do." Really, I do.

V.

BONBON

We called her Bonbon,
Because she was scrumptious like a truffle,
Not a cocoa-powder-dusted dark-chocolate bit of bliss
Housing a cognac-accented ganache—
The kind sold at La Maison du Chocolat—
But a white-chocolate number: a cocoa-butter ball
With a creamy cocoa-butter interior,
So rich, so mmm mmm good.

We called her Bonbon,
Because she was delectably decadent,
Not decadent in the Aubrey Beardsley or
Rome-under-Caligula sense of the word,
But in the peel-me-a-grape,
Indulge-me-to-the-point-of-no-no sense,
Like a water fowl molded from marzipan,
With candied-chestnut eyes and a buttercream bill.

We called her Bonbon,
But one of our crowd proposed Gumdrop,
Thinking back to his boyhood days,
When the more he gobbled handfuls
Of those sticky pectin-based agents of
Dental degeneration, the more they glued
Themselves to his tooth enamel
Like barnacles to a hull.

We called her Bonbon,
Although Jawbreaker was a better fit,
You know, the candy that shows your molars who's boss
And sends your canines scurrying under the living-room couch
With their tail between their legs.
The English call it a gobstopper, gob being Brit-slang for mouth.
We Americans don't go for that fish-and-chips talk.
Jawbreaker says it all. That's right. You got a problem?

The bull dykes in her cellblock call her Bonbon,
Because she gives them sugar, because she oozes
Like a cherry cordial when she does.
They like that.
Her hearing is three weeks from tomorrow.
She'll sail through it, of course. The stars are with her.
The parole board wouldn't deny freedom to anybody
Named Bonbon.

NOUN NOIR

A Fiction

Marriage

Boredom

Infidelity

Widow

Trial

Conviction

Incarceration

Appeal

Failure

Decade

Petition

Hearing

Stay?

Denial

Priest

Penitent

End

HOLY ROGUE!

The poem lists all the villains from the *Batman* TV series (1966-1968) in the order in which they made their first (and sometimes only) appearance.

Season 1

The Riddler[1] equivocated, but finally came clean to
The Penguin[2], who quacked it to
The Joker[3], who guffawed and notified
Mister Freeze[4], who coolly informed
Zelda the Great[5], who pulled it out of her hat for
The Mad Hatter[6], who stole the hat and blabbed to
False Face[7], who was tempted to lie, but was candid with
The Catwoman[8], who purred it to
King Tut[9], who proclaimed it to
The Bookworm[10], who read between the lines and reported it to

Season 2

The Archer[11], who gave it point-blank to
The Minstrel[12], who turned it into a ballad he sang to
Ma Parker[13], who rewrote it as a ransom note she left for
The Clock King[14], who waited an hour before sharing it with
Egghead[15], who may have eggsaggerated a little when he opened up to
Chandell[16], who conveyed it *allegro ma non troppo* to
Marsha, Queen of Diamonds[17], who scintillatingly imparted the knowledge to
Shame[18], who shot his mouth off to
The Puzzler[19], who checked in with Rube Goldberg before he slipped it to
Sandman[20], who slept on it before bringing it to light for
Colonel Gumm[21], who chewed on it before passing it on to
Black Widow[22], who enlightened that absolutely darling little

Season 3

Siren[23], who felt herself caught between a rock and a hard place, but chirped it to
Lola Lasagne[24], who BELTED IT OUT to
Louie, the Lilac[25], who decided to be sweet and advised
Olga[26], who sent a cable to
Lord Marmaduke Ffogg[27] and Lady Penelope Peasoup[28], who wired
Nora Clavicle[29], who made no bones about gossiping to
Calamity Jan[30], who got Shame's permission to spill the beans to
Dr. Cassandra[31] and Cabala[32], who as fast as you can say abracadabra told
Minerva[33], who also heard it from the network executives:
The show's had its run and is officially

Done!

Special Guest Villains and Villainesses

[1] Frank Gorshin

[2] Burgess Meredith

[3] Cesar Romero

[4] George Sanders

[5] Anne Baxter

[6] David Wayne

[7] Malachi Throne

[8] Julie Newmar

[9] Victor Buono

[10] Roddy McDowall

[11] Art Carney

[12] Van Johnson

[13] Shelley Winters

[14] Walter Slezak

[15] Vincent Price

[16] Liberace

[17] Carolyn Jones

[18] Cliff Robertson

[19] Maurice Evans

[20] Michael Rennie

[21] Roger C. Carmel

[22] Miss Tallulah Bankhead

[23] Joan Collins

[24] Ethel Merman

[25] Milton Berle

[26] Anne Baxter

[27] Rudy Vallee

[28] Glynis Johns

[29] Barbara Rush

[30] Dina Merrill

[31] Ida Lupino

[32] Howard Duff

[33] Zsa Zsa Gabor

VI.

THE POLKA-DOT WINGS ADVENTURE

After *Angel*, a 1966 experimental short film by Derek May

The lovely young woman wearing polka-dot wings is happy,
because she's lovely, young, and wearing polka-dot wings.

See how she runs, shaking off the off-white,
waving goodbye to life's flat-blue walls.

The world is a green meadow and every star a baby's breath.
Happiness steps aside for joy. Joy speaks for her.

"I'm not Georgette anymore.
I'm the Woman with Polka-Dot Wings."

*

You need not be lovely or young or female. Your movement need not be pursued by the inquisitive lens/eye of the movie camera. The air around you need not accommodate an instrumental soundtrack by Leonard Cohen.

What is needed is the desire for the happiness that polka-dot wings alone can bring. Out of desire comes determination. Out of determination comes the task.

You will need the following ingredients to see your project to fruition:

- Balsa wood for the frames;
- 15 yards of sheer white fabric;
- 100 orange or violet circular pieces of cloth, each approximately two inches in diameter, 50 per wing;
- Scissors;
- A tape measure;
- A sewing machine;
- A quiet room where no one will disturb your work;
- Uninterrupted time—days or weeks, whichever your constitution and power of concentration demand.

Wear your homemade appendages with pride. Enter the local supermarket and trot down the dairy aisle proclaiming, "I'm not (YOUR NAME) anymore. I'm the (YOUR GENDER) with Polka-Dot Wings."

Do the same in the park, in the mall, in the police station. Preach the Tao of polka-dot wings. Encourage others to leave their cash registers, their keyboards, their spreadsheets and follow you, because you are the Evangelist with Polka-Dot Wings, the Evangelist OF Polka-Dot Wings. Lead your acolytes across bridges and highways during rush hour, so that traffic comes to a standstill and commuters abandon their cars to join the sunny procession. Take them through Maryland, through Missouri, through Oregon.

Be the Forrest Gump of Polka Dot Wings.

THE SWIMMER, STARRING BURT LANCASTER, EMPLOYED AS SEVEN-DAY MEDITATION RITUAL

I. Explanation

This project evolved out of a misreading.

The Philadelphia poet CAConrad, inventor of (Soma)tic poetry exercises, outlines a meditation exercise on his (Soma)tic website (http://somaticpoetrymeditations.blogspot.com/), in which he instructs you to watch one film a day for seven days and each day find something you hadn't seen the previous day. After each viewing, you're to take notes as quickly as you can and use them as the basis for a poem.

When I read "one film a day for seven days," I thought Conrad meant a full-length film of my choice, an ambitious endeavor by any measure. Three days into the project, I realized he's referring to the two- and three-minute videos he filmed and posted on the (Soma)tic web page. Because the (Soma)tic exercise—or my interpretation of it—was underway, I chose to continue as I had begun.

I began on Saturday, April 19, 2014. I spent a good part of the day considering and discounting one film after another, I decided on *Requiem for a Heavyweight* (1962), which would have enabled me to pay tribute to screenwriter Rod Serling, who had a huge influence on me. When I sifted through my collection, however, I couldn't find it. I opted for a film that hadn't crossed my mind until then: *The Swimmer* (1968). Based on a short story by John Cheever, it plays like a 95-minute episode of *The Twilight Zone.*

Burt Lancaster stars as Ned Merrill, an advertising executive who lives in Connecticut. His friends are conspicuously rich. The film opens with Ned ambling through an unspoiled forest, dressed only in bathing trunks. A deer drinks from a stream. A flock of birds takes to the air. Ned arrives at a neighbor's pool and dives in, luxuriating in the glassy water. The husband and wife who own the house, both nursing hangovers, greet Ned enthusiastically and ask him where he's been for so long. He discovers that a sequence of residents' swimming pools forms a "river," which ends at the community pool; he determines that if he swims in each pool, he'd eventually arrive at his house. To his friends' consternation, he makes it his mission to swim home. He collectively calls the swimming pools the Lucinda River after his wife, whom we never see.

As Ned travels from pool to pool, the reception he receives shifts from jovial to hostile to abusive. It becomes evident that each pool visit represents a stage of Ned's life over a period of two years. Something catastrophic happened, but Ned is either oblivious or in denial.

II. Notes

<u>Sunday, April 20</u>

I watched *The Swimmer* in its entirety.

<u>Monday, April 21</u>

I watched *The Swimmer* again.

At the first friends' pool, Ned rhapsodizes about swimming at camp as a child: "We could've swum around the world in those days."

He compares a cloud in the sky to cities as seen from the bow of a ship: Lisbon, Naples, and Istanbul.

"You were a god to me," 20-year-old Julie Hooper tells Ned while they're walking in the meadow. He showed up at the home of her friend's parents, where she and the friend were swimming in the backyard pool.

Ned literally jumps over hurdles as Julie looks on. He's trying to relive his youth. The bad landing and injured ankle remind him he's no longer a master of the universe.

Ned recites a line from the Song of Solomon to Julie: "Thy belly is like a heap of wheat, fenced about with lilies." He tells her, "I'll be your guardian angel."

Ned later meets a blond boy named Kevin Gilmartin Jr. Does Kevin represent Ned as a child?

"People seemed happier when I was a kid," Ned tells Shirley, a stage actress who was—is, he still thinks—his mistress.

<u>Tuesday, April 22</u>

I watched *The Swimmer* in three installments throughout the day.

The early dialogue sounds overly scripted. Ned and his wealthy friends speak in suburban clichés. Ned talks like an English Romantic poet.

I counted the number of pools Ned visits: 10. In *Inferno*, Dante describes nine circles of Hell and the center, where Satan is imprisoned for eternity in ice.

The scene with the boy Kevin has an otherworldly aura. Kevin, playing his recorder, seems like a character from the Greek underworld.

Ned talks about a castle in Ireland to Shirley, who detests him.

In order to get to the community pool—the last pool—Ned has to cross a busy highway. The highway is the threshold. On the other side is the end of his delusion. It's the dividing line between his gold-plated life and the reality he refuses to acknowledge.

Wednesday, April 23

Beginning today and for the rest of the week, I watched *The Swimmer* in smaller segments, dividing my viewing into sets of pool scenes. I spent this day on pools 1 – 3.

Ned is like Adam before the fall from grace. The bathing suit is one step away from unashamed nudity. Wherever he goes, Ned sees Paradise. He comments on the beauty of the sky (aka heaven).

His friends at the first two pools speak to Ned in platitudes that are no different from the niceties one would say to a casual acquaintance. It's all cocktail talk.

When Ned emerges from the third pool, he confronts an older woman, Mrs. Hammar. Her face radiates displeasure, and she demands to know who gave him permission to swim in her pool. Ned reminds her that he's a friend of her son. Mrs. Hammar retorts that Ned never called or visited her son in the hospital. She icily orders him never to set foot on her property again. Ned is perplexed. According to Greek mythology, Zeus struck Phineus blind for misusing the gift of prophecy and sent the Harpies to steal his food. Mrs. Hammar is Ned's Harpy. In his case, Ned is blind to his circumstances; his sustenance is his infatuation with himself.

Thursday, April 24 (Pools 4 – 6)

Time has stood still for Ned. His now is a now no one else recognizes.

Self-delusion is its own damnation. A white-haired man in a white shirt (angel?) tells Ned about a job opportunity (deliverance?). Ned scoffs and walks away when the man mentions a cut in salary.

<u>Friday, April 25 (Pools 7 – 9)</u>

Kevin is selling lemonade. Ned asks for a cup, to which Kevin replies that it costs 10 cents. Charon charged a fee to ferry a soul across the River Styx. Ned asks Kevin if he can use his pool. Kevin takes him to the pool, which his parents have drained because he doesn't know how to swim. Ned says, "I could get down there and make believe I'm swimming across the pool." Ned is on a journey of undesired self-discovery, but prefers to live in a world of make-believe.

Up to this point, Ned has smiled continuously. His teeth are almost a fashion accessory, like an expensive watch. He loses his practiced grin.

"Good Christ, Ned, will you ever grow up?" Shirley sneers when Ned tells her that he's swimming back to his house. Ned embodies the Peter Pan Syndrome long before the term was coined.

"Well, how goes it in Never-Never Land?" Shirley asks contemptuously: another Peter Pan reference.

<u>Saturday, April 26 (Pool 10 and the conclusion)</u>

As he crosses the busy highway, Ned finally looks like someone who's not in control.

Ned is the type of man who once gave orders. He now takes them from the attendants at the community pool. This is his version of Hell.

_____
_____
_____
_____ *

* In deference to readers who haven't seen the film or read Cheever's short story, I removed my interpretation of the surprise ending.

III. Poem

I am an ordinary man. An ordinary man is
free to choose, and I choose the water, and
I swim the water—breaststroke, backstroke,
butterfly stroke—to reach the land and walk
the land to reach the water, and the water is
sweet, like a summer beverage, and the land
is sweet, because the land is the bridge from
the water to the water. I do not look back.

> No, I am not an ordinary man. I am
> a boatman, and I am piloting my boat
> across the water, and the water is clear,
> and my body is the boat, and I am guiding
> my body across the water to the end of the
> water, because I am a boatman, and I am
> piloting my boat, which is my body. I drop
> a nickel in the water and watch its gleaming
> descent. I am paying the water, for safe
> passage to the other side.

No, I am not a boatman. I am a fish—
carp, cod, trout—and I am swimming,
and the water is cool and clean and soothes
my fish body—catfish, paddlefish, pickerel—
and in swimming I am not seeking. I swim
only to swim, because I am a fish—sunfish,
goldfish, red fish, blue fish—and I am in
the water as a fish, swimming. Home.

THE RIVER STYX RECONSIDERED AS A BROOK
FLOWING THROUGH THE BACKYARD
OF A SIX-BEDROOM HOME IN THE SUBURBS

Over tea on the patio
One Thursday morning at ten,
Elise Brookshire thinks about the photo
Of her daughter Margot's old boyfriend
That she found in her husband's wallet.

THE LOUD FAMILY BARES ALL ... AGAIN

**Excavated From TV Archives
By HBO Film *Cinema Verite***

SANTA BARBARA, Calif.   —

We're an American family.
We live in the suburbs.
We have a built-in pool.
My husband doesn't pay attention to me.
He's always on the road for his job.
My wife has a problem.
We raised five children.
Lance moved to New York.
He wants to make it as something or other.
Lance likes boys.
He doesn't like talking to his father.
Grant and Kevin formed a rock band.
Grant thinks he's the next Mick Jagger.
We have two daughters, Delilah and Michele.
The children adore their dad.
My husband is having an affair.
I want a divorce.
We're an American family.
The camera loves us.

WHERE HAVE ALL THE EPITHALAMIUMS GONE?

This house is damned
All inside: damned
The shutters tremble
The garden shrivels
Sparrows flee the attic
Bed sheets squeal
Photographs tear
in their gilt frames
A white dress dies
on the cellar floor
Clocks run sideways
The mirrors go black
The telephones rasp
The faucets whisper
A portrait of a woman
(a comely lady
in her fiftieth year)
flies from the wall
and crashes face down
on the Persian rug
A love seat grows teeth
and devours itself
The living room sighs
This house is damned
God has turned
His back on it
Denies it is part
of His creation
Guardian angels
avert their eyes
and spit
on the
ground
as
they
float
by

THE 1950s B-MOVIE MORALITY PLAY,
OR CREATURE FROM THE BLACK LAGOON,
GRANT US PEACE

Life was too luxurious in the suburbs.
Streets swept virgin-immaculate,
Lawns the envy of the Irish.
Samba rhythms percolated on the stereo.
We were the middle-class Eloi
In split-level tract homes.
We needed those Saturday mornings
With a tarantula the size of Ecuador
To remind us of our good fortune.
Burnt supper? D in arithmetic?
Inconsequential weighed against
An intergalactic raspberry gelatin
Consuming a roadside diner.

In every driveway, a waxed Impala
Or Oldsmobile beamed
Under the Sunday-dinner sun.
Fireworks sequined heaven on the 4th.
Melting ice cream gloved our fingers.
No trace of a radioactive brontosaurus.

Yes, we knew late-night awakenings,
But at least they had nothing to do
With Martian reconnaissance setting up shop
In the field behind the house.
Had we ever noticed how doors slammed
At two a.m. resemble gunshots—
Or something approaching Tokyo from the sea?
The sleepless hours and the rage in the next room
Were only minor inconveniences.
Think of the Incredible Shrinking Man.
Nobody had it worse.

VII.

BIRD-BOY

The child was beautiful. His hair was the color of straw and had the texture of a silk scarf. Below the forelock, which hung like a valance over his brow, were silver-blue eyes, receptacles for all the wonders of the natural world, as one would expect in a child on the eve of his seventh birthday. His body was slender, but his belly had a slight paunch common in younger children.

He was startlingly well mannered, a tribute to his parents' parenting. "Thank you," "Yes, sir," and "No, ma'am" peppered his sentences. His smile was worthy of photographic preservation.

His name was Darrin because his mother loved reruns of *Bewitched*, although Icarus would have made sense if he were a carnival attraction. Darrin, you see, was born without arms, not even stumps. Extending from each shoulder socket—instead of bicep, elbow, forearm, wrist, hand, fingers, and thumb—was a feathered wing. The interior part of the wing was cream white. The posterior side was speckled red and slate gray.

The first word out of his infant mouth wasn't "Dada" or "Mama," but "fly." At that moment, his mother scanned the room for an insect, then saw that her baby was staring out the window at the occupants of the elm tree in the front yard. They, in turn, were looking back at him.

At the tender age of five Darrin made up a tuneless tune, which he sang all the time to his parents' astonishment.

> *Why can't I be like a sparrow and be in the distance away?*
> *Why can't I fly like a sparrow and be as free as he is?*

He sang the song in all its lyrical maturity for show-and-tell in kindergarten. The response of both the teacher and his classmates precipitated the home-schooling decision.

But Darrin was more great auk than oriole. He flapped and flapped and flapped in the hope of defying gravity, but he only jumped.

The night before his birthday, he sat on his bed while his mother gingerly ran a damp washcloth over his wings. She casually asked what he was hoping to get on his birthday. Darrin sang.

Why can't I fly like a sparrow and be as free as he is?

She pressed the cloth against her eyes to keep her young son from seeing her unhappiness. What she heard was not a fabulous wish by an imaginative child, but her flesh and blood's tacit declaration that he felt unloved.

&

She clenched her jaw when he blew out the seven candles on the chocolate chip ice cream cake. She noticed his eyes were closed especially tight when he made his wish. As soon as the tiny flames became wriggles of smoke, she had the sensation of someone waiting in the backyard. She got up from the dining room table and looked out the window. Other than the bushes, trees, and her rose garden, she saw nothing alive. Her husband, spooning the melting confection into Darrin's mouth, asked what the matter was. She ignored him. A sense of presence haunted her. She went downstairs to the back door and opened it. There was the same scene she had observed from the window, but at a different angle. She walked across the hallway to the front door. She pulled it open, and in marched a procession of birds, different kinds of birds—blackbirds, bluebirds, crows, canaries, starlings, thrushes, and, yes, sparrows—in single file, as if they had been in rehearsals for this moment. They hopped up the steps and headed toward the dining room.

Darrin giggled and clapped his wings at the sight of the ambassadors of the air. His father circled the table to install himself between his son and the intruders, but Darrin, even though a youngster, recognized destiny and was glad to surrender to it. He beat his wings furiously. He levitated from his chair and sailed over the table and around his father, generating as much energy as his limited strength and sheer willpower would allow. Blackbirds and thrushes encompassed his mother; crows and bluebirds erected an animate barrier in front of his father. The birds challenged the parents' every move. If she stepped to the left, they stepped to the left. If he moved forward, they spread their wings in unison to cow him, a big multicolored fan of intimidation.

As if he were suddenly autistic, Darrin was unaware that his mother and father were in the room or even that he had a mother and father. His attention was squarely on the creatures that acted with military precision. The birds which were still in line formation led Darrin outside, followed by those that kept his mother and father under close surveillance. His parents, once released, hurried to the door and witnessed the elevation of their only child from a modern freak to a marvel out of Bulfinch's *The Age of Fable*. Darrin was airborne at last, accompanied by his retinue. Their forms became smaller and smaller the further away they flew.

&

She sat stone rigid at the dining room table. The ice cream cake was a mix of misshapen mass and puddle. She heard Darrin singing and first thought he had returned and when she realized he was gone thought her memory was serving as a private jukebox. That wasn't it, either. Darrin's father, wanting a memento of their son's childhood that the boy could experience when he was a teenager or older, had recorded Darrin on an old portable cassette player one evening at bedtime.

> *Why can't I be like a sparrow and be in the distance away?*
> *Why can't I fly like a sparrow and be as free as he is?*

83

VIII.

THEOREMS
For Jenny Holzer

THIS IS EVERYTHING YOU NEED TO KNOW

THIS IS EVERYTHING YOU NEED TO KNOW

THIS IS
EVERYTHING
YOU NEED
TO KNOW

THIS IS EVERYTHING YOU NEED TO KNOW

IX.

THE PERIWINKLE PROJECT

1. Periwinkle is a Crayola® color.

2. *Periwinkle* is a 1917 film starring Mary Miles Minter.

3. Periwinkle is a sea snail, taxonomy *Littorinidae*.

This is concerned with no. 3.

The common periwinkle (*Littorina littorea*) lives along North Atlantic shores. It is not periwinkle (see no. 1).

The blue periwinkle (*Nodilittoria unifasciata*) calls home the waters off the coasts of Australia and New Zealand. As a blue periwinkle, it is a blue periwinkle—with a touch of gray (apologies to the Grateful Dead).

The rough periwinkle (*Littorina saxalitis*) is a littoral jetsetter. It loves Chesapeake Bay, the Barents Sea, and the Strait of Gibralter. This periwinkle, like the common periwinkle, is not periwinkle.

*

Your assignment, should you choose to accept it, is to travel to one of the destinations noted above and for 30 days live in the shallows as a periwinkle.

When you return home, and after you have reacquainted yourself with your terrestrial circumstances and with cooked food, write for submission to *The New York Times Magazine* a 5,000-word article about life inside your shell.

THREE POEMS ON *THE RED BOOK* BY C.G. JUNG[1]

THE DARK SEA BREAKS HEAVILY –
A REDDISH GLOW SPREADS OUT IN IT –
A SEA OF BLOOD FOAMS AT MY FEET

5:15 a.m.	And it is Christ the Sea.
5:25	Sunrise.

I'm thinking of Théodore Géricault's *The Raft of the Medusa*.
The painting depicts the few who survived the inhospitality of the
open sea and the onus of human desperation, who were not
murdered, cannibalized, or driven mad by starvation and hopelessness.

If souls such as these were cast adrift on Christ the Sea,
I believe all would be saved,
that fresh water would come to them,
that bluefish would give their bodies to feed the shipwrecked multitudes.

5:30	I'm alone on the shore.
5:40	I'm not alone on the shore.
	A live manta ray lies yards away, a broken law.
6:05	I'm strolling along a beat-up boardwalk. Its warped, creaking planks no longer know the weight of vacationers' feet. My shoes leave a red trail.
6:15	A second manta ray has joined the one.
6:20	The fun house, the Ferris wheel, the roller coaster, the shooting gallery: The rides and attractions that tenanted the boardwalk are hollow bodies and old men's skeletons. Would the blood tide take them?
6:45	Manta rays are occupying the coast! As far as my eyes allow me to see, I see them advancing millimeter by millimeter by way of their great black Dracula wings to leave Christ the Sea.

Yes.
Of course.
They are also known as devilfish.

---

[1] Kyburz, Mark; John Peck, and Sonu Shamdasani, translators. (New York: W.W. Norton & Co., 2009). The poem titles are quotes from the text.

MAGIC IS A WAY OF LIVING

The magician's arsenal of tricks includes the illusion of making things disappear. The following poem is one poet's variation of the trick. It consists of four individual erasures made from the following paragraph in The Red Book:

Magic is a way of living. If one has done one's best to steer the chariot, and one then notices that a greater other is actually steering it, then magic takes place ... One cannot say what the effect of magic will be, no one can know in advance because the magical is lawless ... Stupidity too is part of this, which everyone has a great deal of, and also tastelessness, which is possibly the greatest nuisance.

Magic is a way of

                                        magic

                        *

Magic

                                                                cannot

say   magic will be   magical

                        *

                                                        because the magical

is lawless

                        *

Magic

                        is   a
                nuisance.

AND I THREW EVERYTHING FROM ME
AND WANDERED TOWARD THE EAST,
WHERE THE LIGHT RISES DAILY

My life is a letter addressed to the East.
My home is the road from the West to the East.

My knapsack is light; I possess myself.
Thus, I walk—at whose behest?—to the East.

An elephant—white!—plodded through my dreams.
I'm the Buddha? Dolt! Take your jest to the East!

My vigor vis-à-vis a monk's is scant.
My backbone is iron. I'm obsessed with the East.

The sun, petulant star, breathes dragon fire.
I, without shame, go undressed to the East.

A hermit wished me Godspeed and said,
"It's done: my long, fruitless quest for the East."

Our common mission in his eyes reposed.
I vowed his name would find rest in the East.

How long have I traveled and what distance?
Surely, it's my lot to be blessed by the East.

My beard is belly long and millstone gray.
Has the East denied my request for the East?

THE MONGOL EMPIRE ENCOUNTER

Greet everybody with a Genghis Khan smile.
Keep it up until somebody inquires,
"Has anyone ever told you that you smile like Genghis Khan?"

X.

POEM FOR MARY SHELLEY

Victor Frankenstein assembled his creature from pieces of corpses. This poem is made up of pieces of works written before 1818, the year Mary Shelley published *Frankenstein*. The cento is meant to reflect her title character's point of view.

Speak, hands, for me![1]
The awful shadow of some unseen Power
Floats though unseen among us.[2]
I had a dream, which was not all a dream.[3]
Man is all symmetry,
Full of proportions, one limb to another,[4]
A brain of feathers, and a heart of lead.[5]

O misery of hell![6]
A little learning is a dang'rous thing.[7]
Fire answers fire.[8]
No man chooses evil because it is evil;
He only mistakes it for happiness.[9]
Science without conscience is
But the ruin of the soul.[10]

---

[1] William Shakespeare, *Julius Caesar*, III, I.

[2] Percy Bysshe Shelley, "Hymn to Intellectual Beauty."

[3] George Gordon, Lord Byron, "Darkness."

[4] George Herbert, "Man."

[5] Alexander Pope, "The Dunciad," Book II.

[6] John Keats, "Endymion."

[7] Alexander Pope, "An Essay on Criticism," Part II.

[8] William Shakespeare, *Henry V*, IV, Prologue.

[9] Mary Wollstonecraft, *A Vindication of the Rights of Men*.

[10] François Rabelais, *Gargantua and Pantagruel*, translated into English 1653-1694 by Sir Thomas Urquhart of Cromarty and Peter Anthony Motteux.

"HIROSHIMA!" I CRIED

Dramatis Personae

Speaker One
Speaker Two
Speaker Three

Speaker One, Speaker Two, and Speaker Three stand side by side before the audience as follows:

> Speaker One, stage right;
> Speaker Two, middle;
> Speaker Three, stage left.

Speaker One and Speaker Three wear white shirts and white slacks. Speaker Two wears a red shirt and white slacks.

Speaker One and Speaker Three lift their heads skyward. Speaker Two's head is bowed. All three extend their arms from their sides, palms up.

The Speakers deliver their lines as if in a trance and at the same pace. The lines are in sets of 23 to represent 8/6/45, the date of the bombing of Hiroshima: 8 + 6 + 4 + 5 = 23. Speaker Two's concluding line, however, is in a set of six to represent the sixth day of August.

Speaker One:

Light heals sin. Light heals sin. Light heals sin.
Light heals sin. Light heals sin. Light heals sin.
Light heals sin. Light heals sin. Light heals sin.
Light heals sin. Light heals sin. Light heals sin.
Light heals sin. Light heals sin. Light heals sin.
Light heals sin. Light heals sin. Light heals sin.
Light heals sin. Light heals sin. Light heals sin.
Light heals sin. Light heals sin.

Speaker One intones a second complete set of "Light heals sin" during Speaker Three's recitation.

Speaker Three:

Light peels skin.
Light peels skin.
Light peels skin.
Light peels skin.
Light peels skin.
Light peels skin.

Light peels skin.
Light peels skin.
Light peels skin.
Light peels skin.
Light peels skin.
Light peels skin.
Light peels skin.
Light peels skin.
Light peels skin.
Light peels skin.
Light peels skin.
Light peels skin.
Light peels skin.
Light peels skin.
Light peels skin.
Light peels skin.
Light peels skin.

SPEAKER ONE and SPEAKER THREE recite, respectively, a third and second set of their lines during SPEAKER TWO's recitation.

SPEAKER TWO:

Light steals kin. Light steals kin. Light steals kin. Light steals kin. Light steals kin.
Light steals kin. Light steals kin. Light steals kin. Light steals kin. Light steals kin.
Light steals kin. Light steals kin. Light steals kin. Light steals kin. Light steals kin.
Light steals kin. Light steals kin. Light steals kin. Light steals kin. Light steals kin.
Light steals kin. Light steals kin. Light steals kin.

SPEAKER ONE falls silent after the third set of "Light heals sin."

SPEAKER THREE falls silent after the second set of "Light peels skin."

The completion of both sets is to be timed to coincide with SPEAKER TWO's twenty-third "Light steals kin." SPEAKER TWO then delivers the closing lines.

SPEAKER TWO:

Light steals kin.
Light steals kin.
Light steals kin.
Light steals kin.
Light steals kin.
Light (*pause*) steals (*pause*) kin.

103

THE PSYCHOTROPIC GHAZAL

Alprazolam, bupropion, clorazepate, ziprasidone,
Buspirone, escitalopram oxalate, ziprasidone.

Amitriptyline, citalopram, pemoline, risperidone,
Clomipramine, imipramine pamoate, ziprasidone.

Amobarbital, donepezil, protriptyline, trazodone,
Doxepin, duloxetine, lithium carbonate, ziprasidone.

Amoxapine, estazolam, oxazepam, quetiapine,
Eszopiclone, fluoxetine, lithium citrate, ziprasidone.

Amphetamine, flurazepam, nortriptyline, sertraline,
Fluvoxamine, lamotrigine, lithium sulfate, ziprasidone.

Aripiprazole, galantamine, loxapine, olanzapine,
Glutethimide, memantine, methylphenidate, ziprasidone.

Atomoxetine, haloperidol, prazepam, quazepam,
Hydroxyzine, mirtazapine, topiramate, ziprasidone.

ENGINES MORE REASONABLE THAN MEN

The title phrase appears in Stanislav Filko's "Associations XXVIII," a list of imagined milestones collectively called "The Future Exploration of the Universe, According to scientists [*sic*]." "Engines more reasonable than men" is a prediction for 2080.

MONDAY

They spend the day pledging their commitment to a balanced budget.

TUESDAY

Reiterating the pledge, they begin.

WEDNESDAY

They congratulate themselves on their dedication and progress.

Work resumes.

THURSDAY

Work continues.

FRIDAY

They achieve a balanced budget.

Acknowledging their obsolescence, they shut down for good.

SATURDAY

They are removed and replaced in preparation for the coming week's agenda.

REASSIGNMENT SURGERY: PATIENT #A-27

Dr. Norris dashes off a flood of notes in his illegible physician's script. Mr. Adams's file is half an inch thick, typical for individuals who apply for the surgery.

Dr. Norris stops writing, even though sentences continue to spout from Adams's mouth like rainwater from a gargoyle. He hands Adams a clipboard and a ballpoint pen. Affixed to the clipboard is a one-page document printed on both sides in eight-point Arial type. Adams's eyes run from the top of the form to the bottom in seconds. Marwick-Sells Memorial Medical Center has entered all his personal information. Adams zeroes in on a box marked "Patient #" above his name.

ADAMS: A-27? What does that mean?

DR. NORRIS: It means you're the 27th individual seeking reassignment surgery from this hospital.

ADAMS: What does "A" stand for? "Applicant"?

DR. NORRIS: If you like.

ADAMS: So, you've done this a total of 26 times.

DR. NORRIS: Twenty-four. We declined two applicants. Their psychological assessments indicated they weren't ideal reassignment candidates.

ADAMS: Okay, you performed the surgery 24 times. May I ask in how many years?

DR. NORRIS: Ten. It's not a common surgery, certainly not as prevalent as transgender surgery, which itself isn't prevalent relative to the entire population. Insurance policies still won't cover it, so only the very wealthy can afford it. But I'm not telling you anything you don't know.

ADAMS: Are the 24 people happy in their new life?

DR. NORRIS: Taking into consideration the long period of adjustment, I would say they are. All except one, that is. He decided after two years he didn't like it at all. He came back and asked for another operation, but reassignment can't be reversed.

Adams resumes reading. Dr. Norris examines the patient's features. Adams, an unmarried trial attorney, could be a model in an advertisement for a law school: wavy brown hair, bedroom eyes, and a tennis player's physique.

He's obviously reconciled himself to the derailment the surgery will do to his lucrative career, Dr. Norris thinks. *But earned or inherited, wealth pays dividends. You could buy a showroom's worth of BMWs for the same price.*

Adams presses the pen over a black line at the bottom of page two. His right hand skitters quickly across the page, leaving a blue signature in its wake. He hands the clipboard and pen back to Dr. Norris, who scribbles on a prescription pad and tears off the top sheet.

DR. NORRIS: Get this filled right away. Take one dose today and three doses daily starting tomorrow.

────────────────────────────────────

An anaesthetized Adams lies on a gurney in the operating room. Dr. Norris, several attendants, and two nurses take their places around him.

DR. NORRIS: Ladies and gentlemen, we are about to perform the initial stage of reassignment surgery. The patient is a 36-year-old Caucasian male in overall good health. Some of you have assisted me in reassignment surgery. For others, it will be a new experience. Today's surgery will be the first of a projected six over the course of 10 to 12 months. Does anyone have any questions?

MULTIPLE VOICES: No, doctor.

DR. NORRIS: If there are no questions, we're ready to begin.

107

DR. NORRIS:	How are you feeling?
ADAMS:	Groggy. Sore.
DR. NORRIS:	The soreness will last a bit. We reconstructed your entire musculature. You're making excellent progress. I'd say textbook progress.
ADAMS:	What time do I go into surgery?
DR. NORRIS:	It ended four hours ago. You made it through your fifth surgery with no complications. You have one more, and your reassignment will be complete, at least the physical part of it.
ADAMS:	When do I go under the knife again?
DR. NORRIS:	Three weeks from tomorrow.

Startled, but enamored of what he sees, Adams gazes at the reflection of the new Adams that confronts him, first, in the full-length mirror the staff brought into his hospital room and, then, in the glass doors and windows he passes as a nurse leads him down the hall to the lobby. *So that's what the A in A-27 stands for*, he thinks. Adams arrives at the reception desk, where Dr. Norris is waiting. The nurse wishes Adams well and leaves him.

ADAMS:	Dr. Norris, you didn't come to see me off, did you?
DR. NORRIS:	I did. I make it a point to say goodbye personally to every reassignment patient.
ADAMS:	You did an excellent job.
DR. NORRIS:	This isn't goodbye. We'll be seeing each other for

follow-up visits for the next few months. Anything you'd like to ask me before you go through those doors?

ADAMS: I don't think so. I think my biggest adjustment is a vegetarian diet.

DR. NORRIS: Your carnivore days are over.

ADAMS: I'm going to miss my lamb chops, but I have to say I have a new appreciation for apples.

DR. NORRIS: I eat one every day. I'm partial to Granny Smiths myself.

ADAMS: You know what they say. An apple a day …

DR. NORRIS: Let's hope not. Well, Mr. Adams, I'm going to say the two words you've waited a year to hear. You're discharged.

ADAMS: Thanks for everything, doctor.

DR. NORRIS: I'll see you next Wednesday. If anything comes up between now and then, you have my number.

Dr. Norris collegially pats Adams on the back of his neck. Because of the scope and duration of these operations, the doctor discovered he acquires an emotional attachment to his patients that never happened in his early years of facelifts. Adams, in turn, has come to look upon Dr. Norris as a friend despite the size of the checks he's made out to Marwick-Sells.

DR. NORRIS: Enjoy your new life, Kevin.

The automatic doors part for Adams. It's mid-morning. The day is overcast and humid. Adams heads down the thousand-foot driveway, which is framed on both sides by exquisitely tended acreage. Maple and dogwood trees line the perimeter of the hospital property. To Adams's right, a groundskeeper steers a riding mower. To his left, a sprinkler system sprays the grass. When he reaches the main road, Adams breaks into a trot. The trot accelerates into a canter. The canter accelerates into a gallop. He races down the center of the street, passing cars, mane whipping behind him in the speed-generated wind, the ripple of the hindquarter muscles visible through the spotted coat. Adams is a picture of strength for the world to see, the pride of the Nez Percé, the very model of a well-bred Appaloosa.

XI.

TWINKLE, TWINKLE (YOUR RADIANT BODY)

For Yayoi Kusama[1]

Imagine yourself as a star. Not in the manner of Daniel Day-Lewis and Joni Mitchell, but as a luminescent orb of hydrogen and helium held together by its own gravity.

Repeat after me:

Sirius
Canopus
Rigil Kentaurus
Arcturus
Vega
Capella
Rigel
Procyon
Achernar
Betelgeuse

Do you like these names? They are, in descending order, the ten brightest stars visible from Earth. Say the names again, this time backwards. Let them become familiar to you. Then, choose two or three of your favorite stars. Pronounce the name of each deliberately and with ardor, as if you fear the star will burn out from a lack of commitment to its being.

Continue until your clothes turn miraculously white.

Continue until glorifying fire bursts from your pores.

Continue until you are Sirius-II,
    you are Arcturus-II,
    you are Betelgeuse-II.

Embrace your nature.

Bring your light to all dark places.

---

[1] This instruction piece was inspired by Kusama's *You Who Are Getting Obliterated in the Dancing Swarm of Fireflies*, Phoenix Art Museum.

Acknowledgments

The author extends his gratitude to the editors of the journals and anthologies where the work in this collection previously appeared.

The Adroit Journal: "Bird-Boy" and "The Walt Whitman Complex"

and/or: "Noun Noir: A Fiction"

Barrow Street: "How to Compose a Sonata for Downtown Express Train"

The Chaffin Journal: "The 1950s B-Movie Morality Play, or Creature from the Black Lagoon, Grant Us Peace"

Echolocation: "The Dark Sea Breaks Heavily – A Reddish Glow Spreads Out in It – A Sea of Blood Foams at My Feet"

Exit Strata: "The Periwinkle Project" and "The Seventh Son of a Seventh Son"

First Literary Review – East: "The Bowery (Not)Sonnet"

Guide to Kulchur Creative Journal: "The Liberace Poem," "The Man-Church Report," "The Psychotropic Ghazal," "*The Swimmer*, Starring Burt Lancaster, Employed as Seven-Day Meditation Ritual," "Theorems," and "Twinkle, Twinkle (Your Radiant Body)"

Harpur Palate: "A Porch Light on a Late Summer Eve"

Hartskill Review: "Deposition: Archaeopteryx"

Italian Americana: "Where Have All the Epithalamiums Gone?"

Lalitamba: "And I Threw Everything from Me and Wandered toward the East, Where the Light Rises Daily"

Liebamour: "The Polka-Dot Wings Adventure"

Maintenant: A Journal of Contemporary Dada Writing & Art: "Engines More Reasonable Than Men"

MARGIE / The American Journal of Poetry: "The River Styx Reconsidered as a Brook Flowing through the Backyard of a Six-Bedroom Home in the Suburbs"

The Más Tequila Review: "Bin-Bin the Dog-Faced Boy" and "The Loud Family Bares All … Again"

The McNeese Review: "Tiny Little Things"

The Nassau Review: "Reassignment Surgery: Patient #A-27"

Nerve Lantern: Axon of Performance Literature: "'Hiroshima!' I Cried" and "It's Always Prime Time"

NYSAI Press: "The Milk Carton Poem"

The Original Van Gogh's Ear: "Poem for Mary Shelley"

PANK: "America's First Telephone Directory, Annotated 132 Years and 50½ Weeks Later"

Petrichor Machine: "Holy Rogue!" and "The Mongol Empire Encounter"

The Rutherford Red Wheelbarrow: "The Third-Floor Prostitutes"

The Same: "Bonbon"

Smartish Pace: "Magic Is a Way of Living"

Soundings East: "I Comfort Crow Jane," under the title "Dear Crow Jane"

Third Wednesday: "The Circus Is Coming to Town"

"Bin-Bin the Dog-Faced Boy," "The Bob Crane Poem," and "The River Styx Reconsidered as a Brook Flowing through the Backyard of a Six-Bedroom Home in the Suburbs" appear in *Flicker and Spark* (Lowbrow Press, 2013).

"The Dark Sea Breaks Heavily – A Reddish Glow Spreads Out in It – A Sea of Blood Foams at My Feet" appears in *A Galaxy of Starfish: An Anthology of Modern Surrealism* (Salò Press, 2016).

"'Hiroshima!' I Cried" appears in *Nuclear Impact: Broken Atoms in Our Hands* (Shabda Press, 2017).

"The Linda Wolfe Poem" appears in *Love Poems* (Frostburg Center for Creative Writing, 2015).

"The Man-Church Report" appears in *Offbeat/Quirky* (Offbeat/Quirky Books, 2017).

"Poem for Mary Shelley" and "The Polka-Dot Wings Adventure" appear in *Meta-Land: Poets of the Palisades II* (The Poet's Press, 2016).

www.ingramcontent.com/pod-product-compliance
Lightning Source LLC
Chambersburg PA
CBHW080842250626
47161CB00010B/3163